For Oliver and Daniel Downing
~ G P J

SQUARE
FISH

An Imprint of Macmillan

Square Fish books may be purchased for business or promotional use.
For information on bulk purchases, please contact the Macmillan Corporate
and Premium Sales Department at (800) 221-7945 x 5442 or by
e-mail at specialmarkets@macmillan.com.

Library of Congress Cataloging-in-Publication Data Available
ISBN 978-1-250-02932-4 (paperback) / 978-1-250-04507-2 (ebook)

Originally published in Great Britain by Stripes Publishing
First Square Fish Edition: April 2013
Square Fish logo designed by Filomena Tuosto
mackids.com

2 4 6 8 10 9 7 5 3

HOLLYWOOD SHOWDOWN

GARETH P. JONES

SQUARE
FISH

NEW YORK

The story you hold in your hands takes place in the glamorous world of Hollywood—home to the movies, and their stars. Which got me thinking about these words, penned by the great romantic poet Theo Dovelove:

Oh, how I long for glamour and glitz. Instead I've a headache and a bad case of nits.

Theo was a vole, who often appeared on the cover of *Furry Poet Pinups*. You could say he was a *vole model*. What is the point of me telling you this? I have no idea. Really, I should be introducing you to the Clan of the Scorpion . . .

Four ninja meerkats, all fearless warriors, ever willing to risk their lives in order to

save our planet from its most dangerous
enemy, the Ringmaster.

Jet Flashfeet: a super-fast ninja whose
only fault is craving the glory
he so richly deserves.

Bruce "the muscle"
Willowhammer: the
strongest of the gang,
though in the brain race he
lags somewhat behind.

Donnie Dragonjab: a
brilliant mind, inventor, and
master of gadgets.

Chuck Cobracrusher: his clear
leadership has saved
the others' skins more
times than I care to remember.

Oh, and me, Grandmaster
One-Eye: as old and wise as the sand dunes
themselves.

You may recall that in their last adventure, the Clan learned that their deadly foe, the Ringmaster, was somewhere on the West Coast of America. As we catch up with them now, they have just arrived at Los Angeles International Airport, not far from Hollywood itself, which brings to mind another of Theo's poems:

My favorite movies are action-packed,
with excitement and big laughs.
But I don't like those in black and white,
or films about giraffes.

But now it's time for the story of . . .
HOLLYWOOD SHOWDOWN.

CHAPTER ONE

OLD DOGS, NEW TRICKS

Hundreds of planes arrive at Los Angeles International Airport every day, bringing tourists from around the world to the city. They come to soak up sunshine, glamour, and excitement, and to visit the city's most famous district: Hollywood. It was on one such plane that Chuck, Donnie, Jet, and Bruce (otherwise known as the Clan of the Scorpion) had arrived, hidden in an overhead luggage compartment. They were now making their way across the airport arrivals hall, heading for the exit.

You might think that four ninja meerkats walking through a bustling airport would cause something of a stir. But the Clan moved around undetected, thanks to one of Donnie's cunning disguises. As far as the humans were concerned, all they could see was a child in a pair of baggy jeans and a hooded top. Inside the outfit, however, were four meerkats, balanced on each other's shoulders.

Bruce Willowhammer, the strongest of the team, was at the bottom of the pile, and had his furry feet strapped to a pair of stilts. On his shoulders were Jet Flashfeet and Donnie Dragonjab, whose trademark bag of gadgets was strapped to his back. Jet and Donnie were each operating one of the child disguise's arms, opening doors, pressing elevator buttons, and, at one point, batting away an over-friendly dog. At the top of the stack was Chuck Cobracrusher, the leader of the group, his face hidden inside the hooded top.

The only problem with this arrangement was that it meant Bruce was in control of where the Clan went.

And Bruce was easily distracted.

As he strode across the arrivals hall, he peered through a pair of eyeholes at the top of the jeans. "Hey, that's Vin Pain!" he exclaimed, spotting a TV screen showing an entertainment news program. He quickly changed direction and headed for the TV.

"Bruce, remember our mission," warned Chuck. "We need to find out where the Ringmaster is, and what he is up to!"

"Who's Vin Pain?" asked Jet, folding down a specially designed pocket flap in the hoodie so he could see the TV too.

"Sounds like something you'd tell the doctor about," said Donnie. "Ooh, I've got a nasty Vin Pain all down my back."

"Who's Vin Pain?" exclaimed Bruce. "Only the best action hero in the world, that's who! Haven't you seen *Blown to Pieces*? What about *The Smash-up Man* or *Big Guns and Loud Bangs*? Brilliant films. Some of them are really clever too."

The TV showed a clip from a film in which Vin Pain was jumping across the tops of cars hurtling down a busy highway, while dodging a storm of bullets that rained down on him from a helicopter.

"Yeah, looks *really* clever," said Donnie sarcastically.

"Bruce, we do not have time to watch TV right now. We need to keep moving," Chuck called down.

"Vin does all his own stunts and everything," said Bruce, ignoring Chuck.

"Ha," snorted Jet. "I bet he can't do a Super Looping Somersault Leap. That's my new move. I read about it in *How to Flatten Your Enemies and Beat People*."

"Shhh!" said Bruce. "Vin's about to say his trademark line."

On the screen, a building burst into flames for no good reason. Standing in front of it, the muscle-bound star turned to the camera and said in a gruff voice, "Things are getting rough around here . . . so I'm about to get tough."

"Brilliant," said Bruce, clapping his paws excitedly, causing the others to wobble precariously above him.

Chuck tutted. "The Way of the Scorpion teaches us not to engage in such showy displays. Calmness and serenity are our goals. We should only lift a paw to fight when we have no other choice."

"Actually, that was pretty cool, Chuck," said Jet.

"Why does everything always burst into flames in Hollywood films?" sighed Donnie.

On the TV, a female reporter with alarmingly white teeth filled the screen.

"Action hero Vin Pain is used to saying how things are *getting rough*, but in Vin's next film it's a case of things *going woof*." She smirked, then continued. "Why? Because Vin's new co-star is a dog. Her name? Doris the Dancing Dog." The screen showed the familiar face of Doris, the Ringmaster's faithful canine companion.

"So, Doris is a movie star now," said Chuck. "Most interesting..."

The picture changed to show Doris having her photo taken alongside Vin Pain on the red carpet at a film premiere.

"The film's title is a closely guarded secret and very little is known about the canine newcomer," continued the reporter, "except that she is currently being trained at the Real Academy of Dog Actors, or RADA for short. The acting school is run by celebrity dog-trainer Honor Longlead, who joins us now."

The TV showed another smiling woman with equally white teeth.

"So, Honor," said the reporter, "is Doris the Dancing Dog a superstar in the making?"

"Absolutely. Doris is a very talented pup," she replied. "She's been circus trained, but you should see her during the fight scenes. She's a natural."

"I bet she is," muttered Jet. The Clan of the Scorpion had come up against Doris on more than one occasion and had the scars to prove it.

"Well, we look forward to seeing her in action! Thanks, Honor. That's it for this week's edition of *Hollywood Spotlight*. Or should I say, *Holly*woof *Spotlight*?" The presenter smiled and moved on to the next item. "Coming up after the break, we'll be discussing why the U.S. president flew into L.A. this morning along with his super-cute pet sausage dog, Chip O'Lata. Some are saying it's a popularity-boosting trip before the beginning of election season next month . . ."

Bruce turned away from the screen and headed for the exit.

"Well, Bruce, it would appear that your love of film has given us our first lead," said Chuck, "and it is a *dog* lead. We will head straight for this acting school. The Ringmaster is sure to be behind Doris's newfound fame, so he won't be far away . . ."

"Can we go and see where Vin made *Dynamite for Dinner* later? And the sequel, *Destruction for Dessert*?" asked Bruce.

"Once we have defeated the Ringmaster, perhaps," Chuck replied. "Until then, we must be like movie cameras, and stay focused."

CHAPTER TWO

RADA

Outside the airport, dozens of people lined up for buses and taxis to take them into the city. Bruce weaved his way down the pavement, trying not to bump into anyone.

"RADA is located in the Hollywood Hills," said Donnie, looking up the address on his specially modified smartphone.

"Great. Which way do we go?" said Jet.

"North, but this city is far too big to get there on foot," Donnie replied.

"I have an idea," said Chuck. "Bruce, head for that blue bus."

"Can't we get something to eat first?"
asked Bruce, making his way toward the
bus, which had the words ALL ACCESS
HOLLYWOOD STAR TOURS on its side.
"How about a hot dog, or a hamburger,
a bag of popcorn, some French fries . . ."

"Bruce, you must learn to think with
something other than your stomach,"
said Chuck.

"Why?" said Donnie. "It *is* the biggest
organ in his body."

"Hey, I may get hungry, but I've never
eaten anything as big as an organ,"
complained Bruce. He joined the line that
had formed by the bus.

The door opened and a red-faced man
with a huge smile appeared.

"Welcome to the All Access Hollywood
Star Tour, the quickest, easiest, and cheapest
way to soak up the glamour of Hollywood!"

he shouted. "I'm Duane Schneebly, your driver and host. Please hand your tickets to me as you get on board."

"We haven't got a ticket," whispered Jet.

"Leave it to me," said Chuck.

"Can I see your ticket, son?" Duane asked when they reached the front of the line and clambered up the steps of the bus.

"My mother's got it—she's already on board," said Chuck, making no effort to sound like a child. "Will you be visiting RADA today?"

"We sure will." Duane peered down at the hooded boy. "Where are you from, kid? I can't place your accent."

"A secret location in a remote part of the Red Desert," Chuck replied.

"Oh, riiight . . ." Duane smiled and patted Chuck on the head. "Go on, you go find your mama now."

The meerkats found a seat at the back of the bus. They waited until the tourists were distracted by the bus pulling out of the station before stealthily climbing out of their disguise. The bus headed toward central Los Angeles, driving down busy, broad highways lined with billboards promoting the latest movies and biggest TV shows. But the meerkats missed all of this, remaining hidden under the seats at Chuck's insistence.

"Can't I have a quick peek out of the window?" said Bruce. "I'll be really careful."

"No, it is too risky," said Chuck.

As the bus drove into the district of Hollywood itself, past dozens of fast-food venues and huge shopping malls, Duane kept the passengers amused with stories about famous people he had met and movies that had been filmed in the city. When they pulled up outside an elaborate

Chinese building, he explained that this was a cinema where all the biggest stars had their hands and footprints pressed into the concrete paving stones outside. He brought the bus to a halt and everyone climbed off to have a look around. Bruce immediately scooted about under the seats, looking for discarded snacks.

CRUNCH!
CRUNCH!

Captain Chedda's Cheesy Puff Snacks

"Bruce," said Chuck, watching him tuck into a packet of chips. "As ninjas trained in the Way of the Scorpion, we should not pollute our bodies with junk food."

"We're meerkats," replied Bruce. "We have a diet of insects, worms, and lizards. How much worse can Captain Chedda's Cheesy Puff Snacks be?"

When the passengers got back on board, the tour continued.

"Next, ladies and gentlemen," Duane announced, "we're going to head up into the Hollywood Hills, home to many of our brightest stars."

Donnie followed their progress using the GPS map on his phone. They turned off the wide, palm-tree-lined boulevard and onto a narrower, winding road that led up a hill. The houses were bigger and more spectacular here.

"If you look to your right you'll get a great view of the world-famous Hollywood sign," said Duane.

"I've got to get a photo," said Donnie, switching his phone to camera mode.

"No, Donnie—we must remain hidden," said Chuck.

Donnie sighed and put his phone away.

"Hey, folks," said Duane, suddenly sounding excited. "Now, this is a treat—a real celebrity! Look to your left, through those gates, and you'll see Hollywood tough guy Vin Pain outside his home!"

"What?" exclaimed Bruce. Without thinking, he leaped up to look through a window, right in front of an elderly lady who had been trying to take a photo.

"Ahh! A filthy rat!" she screamed.

"That's not a rat. It's a chipmunk," said the man behind her.

"No, it's a squirrel," another lady cried.

"Time to go," Chuck said. "Come on, Bruce."

The terrified tourists lifted their feet in horror as the meerkats ran beneath their seats; one man even tried to swat them with a rolled-up newspaper.

When they reached the front of the bus, Bruce delivered a sharp kick to the door, and the Clan of the Scorpion leaped to freedom. They hurried up the pavement and took cover behind a large fern outside Vin Pain's mansion.

"Please remain calm, folks," they heard Duane plead, before the door hissed shut and the bus pulled away.

"Bruce, you must learn to control your excitement," scolded Chuck.

But Bruce wasn't listening. "Look!" he said, pointing.

On the other side of the gates, Vin Pain was opening the door of a large black car.

"Wow," gasped Donnie. "A stretch limo,

custom-made from a Chevrolet Corvette Stingray. There are only a few of those in the world."

"Forget about the car—look who's with Vin," said Jet.

A shadowy figure, wearing a tailcoat and top hat, had emerged from Vin's house, and was walking toward the limousine.

"The Ringmaster," Chuck growled.

CHAPTER THREE

DOBERMAN SECURITY

As the car moved toward the gates, the meerkats strained to see inside, but the limo's windows were made of tinted glass, hiding the passengers and driver from view.

"We can't let them get away," said Jet.

"Like a boy band that has outgrown its appeal, it is advisable that we split up at this point," said Chuck. "Two will follow the Ringmaster. Two will go to RADA."

"Please can I follow Vin?" begged Bruce.

"Very well," said Chuck. "I shall accompany you. Donnie and Jet, see if you can track down Doris at RADA."

The meerkats waited for the automatic gates to open. Then, as the limo drove past, Bruce and Chuck broke cover. They leaped out from behind the fern and sprinted after it, jumping up onto the car's bumper as it cruised down the hill.

Jet and Donnie watched as the limo disappeared down the road. "So how do we find this dog school?" Jet asked.

Donnie pulled out his phone and showed him the map. "This is where we are and this is where we're going. It's only a few streets away."

"What about a disguise? Can we use the hoodie boy again?"

"Not with just two of us. But luckily, I have just the thing—it's my new and improved Prototype Undercover Pretend Poodle Yoodle disguise, aka P.U.P.P.Y."

From his backpack, he pulled out a dog costume that Jet had last seen on their adventure in Hong Kong.

"What's new about that?"

"Well, I've adapted it so it can be operated by two of us. And then, of course, there's these..." said Donnie, pulling out two pairs of roller skates. "No more walking for us. We're freewheeling all the way there."

✦ ✦ ✦

Anyone in the Hollywood Hills who looked out of their window that afternoon would have seen a roller-skating dog zooming past. But then Hollywood is the sort of place where anything can happen, and a roller-skating dog isn't exactly newsworthy.

"This is really cool, Donnie," said Jet, who was in the back of the poodle disguise.

"No, it's *wheely* cool," Donnie replied, weaving in and out of the palm trees that lined the sidewalk.

After a few minutes, they arrived at a large gate with a sign that read RADA: THE REAL ACADEMY OF DOG ACTORS. Through the gate they could see a white-pillared mansion surrounded by expansive gardens.

"We'll have to sneak in through the gates," said Jet.

"Wait," said Donnie. "Look, security cameras. We need to get in without being seen and that means getting over the wall. Come on, over here."

They slipped behind a palm tree and changed out of the dog disguise. Donnie rifled around in his backpack and pulled out a long piece of elastic. He handed one end to Jet and told him to tie it around the tree trunk as high up as possible. Donnie tied the other end to a nearby tree.

"I call this my meerkat-apult," he said.

They stood side by side in front of the elastic and walked backward until it would stretch no farther.

"On my count, jump," said Donnie. "One, two, three . . . NOW!"

"Wait!" Jet cried. "The poodle disguise! It's still under the treeeee..."

WHOOOOSH!

But it was too late. The elastic flung them into the sky and over the wall. The pair landed inside the grounds of RADA behind a hedge.

They could hear barking coming from a row of kennels alongside the mansion.

"Dogs are crazy, always making so much noise," said Jet. "You mean, they're barking mad," replied Donnie. "Right, time to look around. We'll use the dog disguise."

"You mean the dog disguise that we just left behind the tree on the other side of that wall?" asked Jet.

"Ah. Yes. What else have I got in here . . ." Donnie opened his bag and rooted around inside. "We'll have to use the cat disguise."

"What?" Jet exclaimed. "Dress up as a cat in a place full of dogs? Isn't that like going to a lion convention dressed as a zebra?"

"Better that than risk Doris recognizing us," said Donnie, pulling a fluffy white cat costume from his bag. "Besides, these are acting dogs, they probably have to work with cats all the time."

Reluctantly, Jet slipped into the back half of the cat, and Donnie climbed into the front.

They rounded the hedge and were about to investigate when Donnie came to a halt. "Hang on," he said, "the gate's opening."

They watched as a line of five black Cadillac limousines pulled up. The cars came to a halt in front of the main house, and a dozen men in suits stepped out. They were all wearing sunglasses and discreet earpieces, and Donnie caught a glimpse of a gun holster at one man's hip.

"What's going on?" asked Jet. "I can't see anything back here."

"Security men," said Donnie. "There must be someone important in one of those limos." He paused for a moment. "Yes, a tall, smartly dressed man has just climbed out of the middle car. He's carrying a little brown sausage dog."

"What's happening now?" asked Jet.

"Honor Longlead is coming out to greet the man. I can't hear what they're saying, but they're going inside. Let's take a closer look."

Donnie and Jet padded toward the
main building as casually as they could
manage, considering they were dressed as
a cat and there were armed security men
everywhere they looked. They slipped down
the side of the building and jumped up
onto a window ledge. Peering inside, they
saw the tall man from the car deep in
conversation with Honor Longlead. The
sausage dog was on the floor, and next to
it was Doris the Dancing Dog.

"It's so kind of you to give Chip this
acting lesson, Miss Longlead," said the man.

"Please call me Honor. And it's no
problem at all, Mr. P—"

The man interrupted her. "I'd much
rather you call me Jim. Chip's awfully
nervous, this being his first film role. If I'm
honest, I'm a bit nervous myself, getting to
meet Vin Pain. When the director contacted

me and offered Chip this role, I couldn't believe my luck. I'm Vin's biggest fan!"

Honor Longlead smiled. "I imagine he's more nervous about meeting *you*."

At that moment, Jet felt a tug on the tail of the cat costume. "What the—" he started, but before he could say another word, he and Donnie were hauled off the ledge and thrown to the ground.

"Well, howdy," a voice drawled. "You're a funny-looking dog."

Standing over them was a huge Doberman. Globules of spit hung from his sharp teeth as he flashed them a sinister grin.

"I was just patrolling these grounds," the dog continued, "you know, keeping everything nice and secure, when I saw you standing there on the ledge. And I thought to myself, 'Bud,' I thought, 'that is a funny-looking dog. So funny, I'd say it looks more like a cat. And if that's a cat,' I thought, 'I'd be authorized to use force to get it off these premises, what with me being responsible for security here.'"

"We're not a cat," said Jet as he and Donnie clambered to their feet inside the costume.

"*We?*"

"He means 'I'," said Donnie. "*I* mean 'I'. *I'm* not a cat. I'm a dog."

Bud looked confused. "A dog? What breed of dog-gone dog would you be then?"

"I'm a . . . long-tailed Egyptian spaniel," said Donnie, hoping that if such a dog did exist, Bud had never seen one.

"Very rare," added Jet.

"Really? Well, there is *one* way to make sure you're telling the truth," said Bud. "If I take a bite, I can see whether you taste of cat. I sure like the taste of cat."

"Now now, there's no need for that . . ." said Donnie, backing away.

"Just a small bite for starters," said Bud. As he lunged and sank his teeth into the middle of the cat costume, Donnie and Jet leaped out of it to avoid the razor-sharp teeth.

RIIIIP!

There was a ripping sound, and when Bud looked up, there were two meerkats standing before him. Beside them on the ground lay two halves of the empty cat costume.

"What *are* you?" Bud asked with a snarl.

"We're ninja meerkats," said Donnie proudly.

"Did you say *cats*?"

"No, *meer*kats," said Jet, drawing his nunchucks.

"Sounds to me like you're saying *me a cat*. Well, *me a dog* and so are my boys. Here, boys!" Bud barked.

Nine more drooling Dobermans stepped out from behind the bushes.

"What d'you reckon, Jet?" said Donnie.

"I think it's time for some ninja action," replied Jet.

The dogs snarled and charged at them.

With perfect timing, Jet shot into the air, causing two of the dogs to smash into the wall behind him, then sent another reeling with a THWACK from his nunchucks. "Now for my new move," he announced. "The Super Looping Somersault Leap."

Using one of the Doberman's heads as a springboard, Jet shot into the air and performed a spectacular quadruple somersault. Unfortunately, however, he landed directly back where he had started . . . except now his hind feet were keeping the dog's jaws open. One false move and he'd be facing a slobbery end.

"Oops," said Jet. "That wasn't quite what was supposed to happen. Can you lend us a paw, Donnie?"

"Hey, Dopey Doberman, if you fancy a snack, try this," cried Donnie, reaching into his bag and pulling out a large bone. Jet dived out of the way as the dog jumped up and snatched the bone between its teeth.

Donnie grinned. "Ha! That's coated in super-fast drying glue. And it looks like it's worked already."

The dog growled angrily, but its teeth were stuck fast.

"Watch out!" yelled Jet, spotting another Doberman racing toward Donnie. Jet jumped to his feet and landed an almighty roundhouse kick on the dog's left cheek, sending him sprawling.

"Ninja-boom!" he cried.

But now the meerkats had a new problem—the fight had attracted the attention of the security men, who were running over from inside the mansion.

"We've got to get out of here," said Donnie.

"Well, we won't get far unless we lose these dogs first," Jet said, knocking another Doberman off his feet with a leg sweep.

Donnie reached into his bag and pulled out a crossbow and a second sticky bone.

"I call this my cross-bone," he explained.

"Get a move on, will you?" Jet cried.

"All right, all right." Donnie loaded the weapon, then whistled loudly. "Hey, you mangy mutts! It's dinnertime!"

He squeezed the trigger, and the remaining four Dobermans sprinted after the flying bone.

"Great! Now, you got another fancy gadget to get us back over that wall?" asked Jet.

"Nope—for that we use our natural ability." He held up his paws and flexed his claws. "We burrow."

The meerkats turned and sprinted back to the wall. Within seconds, they'd dug down under it and disappeared, leaving the confused security men and Dobermans in a cloud of dust.

CHAPTER FOUR

EVIL PLOTS & GOOD DOGS

Meanwhile, in another part of the city, the large black limousine carrying Vin Pain and the Ringmaster glided down a wide street. Bruce and Chuck scrambled up the back window and onto the roof, moving quickly to avoid being spotted.

"This is amazing," Bruce whispered. "I can't believe we're so close to Vin Pain!"

"Do not forget that the car also contains the Ringmaster," replied Chuck.

They peeked through the sunroof. It was impossible to hear what was being said, but Vin was holding a document in his hands with the words "EVIL PLOTS" written on it in large black letters. Something else was written underneath, but it was obscured by his huge thumbs.

"Do you think I can get Vin's autograph later?" asked Bruce.

"Bruce, your hero is sitting next to our deadliest enemy, reading a document entitled 'Evil Plots'," said Chuck. "It may well be that Vin Pain is in league with the Ringmaster."

"No way," said Bruce. "He's probably just undercover like he was in that film, *Undercover Good Guy*. Vin says he'll only ever play good guys because he knows he's a role model to millions."

"The words of celebrities are like boiled eggs," said Chuck, "best taken with a pinch of salt."

The car turned into the parking lot of a fancy-looking restaurant and drew to a halt. Chuck and Bruce slipped down to the ground, and hid behind one of the wheels as the Ringmaster and Vin stepped out.

". . . It's a great idea. It'll really get people talking," Vin was saying.

"Oh yes, this will certainly get everyone talking," the Ringmaster replied.

"Should we follow them?" asked Bruce.

Chuck shook his head. "Too risky. But I think they left the document in the car. Can you open the sunroof?"

"No problem," said Bruce.

"Remember, the driver's still inside," Chuck pointed out. "We must be as silent as mute mice playing charades in a library."

They scurried back up to the roof and Bruce wedged his claws under the edge of the sunroof and forced it open. Chuck dropped down inside, while Bruce remained where he was, holding the sunroof.

"Good work, Bruce. I will only be a minute," Chuck whispered. He picked up the document, which was lying facedown on the seat, and flipped it over.

EVIL PLOTS & GOOD DOGS

He opened it to the first page.

ACT ONE: SCENE ONE
Interior of a circus tent.

"It appears to be a script," said Chuck.

"It must be Vin's new film," exclaimed Bruce excitedly. He dropped down into the car to take a look.

The sunroof slid shut.

"Oops," said Bruce.

Suddenly, the limo lurched forward and both meerkats lost their balance as it sped out of the parking lot and away down the street. Chuck rattled the door handle. It was locked. "Try the windows," he ordered.

In an attempt to shatter one of the windows, Bruce threw himself against the glass, but bounced off like a furry rubber ball.

"Ow!" he said, rubbing his shoulder.

"Hey uh, Grimsby, the meerkat's hurt himself on the window," said a familiar voice.

"That'll be what they call *window pain*," replied another, chuckling.

A TV screen set into the panel dividing the back of the limo from the front seat flickered to life, showing the Ringmaster's two evil clown henchmen, Grimsby and Sheffield. Grimsby was driving, while Sheffield sat beside him.

The limousine swerved violently to the right, throwing the meerkats against the left-hand door.

"Your driving is even worse than your jokes," said Chuck.

"We thought you might come along to crash the party at some point," said Grimsby. "And here you are!"

"It's a good thing this car alerts us when the sunroof's been opened," said Sheffield.

"And it's a good job that there's no way out, now that we've locked the doors."

"The Ringmaster was fuming when you survived his snow bomb at Ice Mountain," Grimsby added. "He'll be so pleased to hear that we ran into you now, before his plan really kicks into gear." With that, he swung the limo around another sharp corner, flinging the meerkats to the other side of the car.

"What is the Ringmaster plotting this time?" demanded Chuck. "And what's the meaning of this film script?"

"It's going to be a smash hit, that one," said Grimsby. "Speaking of which . . ."

The limo came to a sudden halt. Chuck and Bruce grabbed hold of the door handles to avoid flying forward.

"It's time for your crushing defeat," said Sheffield.

The screen went blank and the meerkats could hear the clowns' laughter as they got out of the limo. Bruce climbed up onto the seat and looked through the window. "I think we're in some kind of scrapyard," he said. They were surrounded by beaten-up old cars, stacked like building blocks.

Chuck joined him at the window. "We must find a way out," he said.

There was a loud CLUNK from above, and the limo jolted, knocking the meerkats over again. This was followed by a rocking motion, as the limo was lifted into the air.

The meerkats scrambled to their feet.

"We're flying!" exclaimed Bruce.

"No, we're being lifted," said Chuck.

The limo swung around, allowing them to see that they were moving toward a large steel machine that was crushing cars into cubes.

Chuck pulled out his phone and switched it to loudspeaker. "I'm calling Donnie. He knows all about this car. Perhaps he can tell us how to get out."

Donnie answered the phone on the second ring. "Hi, Chuck. What's up?"

"Donnie, we're trapped inside the back of the limo and are about to be crushed. How can we get out?" said Chuck urgently.

"Ah. I hate to say it, but there's no way out of that thing," said Donnie. "It's got bulletproof glass and a reinforced body—that car is like a prison on wheels."

"There must be *something* we can do," Chuck replied, as the limo swung closer to the huge crushing-machine.

"Well, it is an electric vehicle," Donnie conceded. "I suppose if you were to short-circuit the electricity, that might unlock all the doors."

"How would we do that?" asked Chuck.

"You'd need to pour water down the back of the seat. The car's circuit board should be housed there."

Bruce opened the refrigerator compartment and pulled out a bottle of mineral water.

"Got some!" he said.

"Pour it down the back of the seat—quick!" shouted Chuck.

Bruce followed orders, and emptied the contents of the bottle.

The sound of glass shattering and metal being crushed was deafening. The limo was now dangling directly over the huge jaws of the machine. In seconds, the car and everything in it would be squashed into a small metal cube.

"What now?" Bruce roared.

"Try the doors!" Chuck shouted back.

Bruce rattled the handle.

"It's not working!" cried Chuck.

"It might take a couple of minutes to work," said Donnie.

"We don't have—"

The end of Chuck's sentence was cut off by a click, thump, CRUNCH!

"Chuck! Bruce? What's happening?" Donnie shouted on the other end of the phone. But no one answered.

CHAPTER FIVE

SCRAPYARD CHALLENGE

What Donnie didn't know was that with seconds to spare, the car door had unlocked, and Chuck and Bruce had leaped to safety. Chuck had grabbed the film script, but dropped his phone in the process, leaving it to be crushed inside the limousine.

"Now, where are those clowns?" Bruce growled, dusting himself off. "I'll teach them to mess with us."

"I'm afraid that lesson may have to wait. Look," said Chuck, nodding at the exit to the scrapyard just as the clowns zoomed through it on a motorbike.

"Should we go after them?" asked Bruce.

"No, if they think we've been crushed, we will have the element of surprise on our side next time we meet," said Chuck. "Now we must let Donnie and Jet know that we're OK, and tell them what we've found out. Bruce, have you got your phone?"

"No, mine stopped working after I broke an egg on it."

Chuck frowned. "Why would you break an egg on your phone?"

"Because I thought Donnie said you could *fry* on it, but it turned out he said you could get *Wi-Fi* on it," Bruce explained. "And that doesn't involve eggs, apparently. Ooh, I could eat a plate of eggs right now . . ."

"We must find a way to contact the others," said Chuck. "Follow me."

They hurried over to a shack at the

center of the scrapyard. The meerkats slipped through the open door and hid behind a wastepaper basket, unnoticed by the two men inside.

One was leaning back in his chair, scratching his belly and watching television, while the second man stood over him, shouting.

"Tony, who told you to put that limo through the crusher?"

"Those two clowns, boss."

"What? The clowns who just stole my motorbike?"

"Yeah, them," Tony yawned. "They paid in cash and said it was urgent."

His boss rolled his eyes, exasperated. "A couple of guys you've never met turn up

in disguise and ask you to crush a car, and
that didn't strike you as suspicious?"

"They weren't in disguise, boss. They're
clowns."

"*You're* the clown," said the other man.
"Now come on, we've got to get after those
thieves! I'll call the cops from the car."

Tony reluctantly got up and followed his
boss out.

Chuck and Bruce scrambled out from
behind the wastepaper basket
and jumped up onto the
desk. Chuck picked up
the phone and
dialled Donnie's
number.

"Chuck! Are
you OK?" asked
Donnie.

"Yes, thanks to you," Chuck replied. "What did you learn at RADA?"

"Well, there was a man there with a lot of security and a sausage dog called Chip that also seems to be in this film with Vin and Doris," said Jet.

"Hmm. Chip . . . that name sounds familiar," said Chuck. "We have learned that the Ringmaster is involved in making the film, but we are not sure what his plan is. Can you get here as soon as possible? We need your inventive genius, Donnie."

Chuck found the scrapyard's address on a letter on the desk, read it out, then hung up.

"Hey, look, it's that dog-trainer woman again," said Bruce, pointing at the TV.

Chuck turned up the volume, and both meerkats watched the footage of Honor Longlead shaking hands with a tall, smartly dressed man.

"Hollywood insiders say that Chip O'Lata, the president's pet sausage dog, has landed a role in a major movie," said a reporter.

"The president's dog! Of course, I thought I had heard that name before," said Chuck. "But like a jigsaw puzzle short of a piece, the picture is still not clear."

When the news feature ended, Chuck and Bruce waited for the others in the deserted scrapyard. Chuck found a spot where he could sit and meditate, while Bruce avidly read the film script, occasionally muttering things like, "Cool," or, "That'll look amazing."

By the time Jet and Donnie arrived in their poodle costume on wheels, Bruce had finished reading. "This is going to be a fantastic film," he told them. "And I know where they're going to make it—the studio's address is written on the last page."

Chuck smiled. "Very good. Then that is where we shall go. We are not all going to fit into the poodle costume, so we will need a different form of transportation. Donnie, do you think you can whip up something?"

"In a scrapyard like this?" Donnie replied. "Let the hammering commence!"

☆　☆　☆

It didn't take long for Donnie to get an old hot-dog van (complete with a huge plastic hot dog on top) working again. With Bruce's help he fitted new tires, and got Jet to screw them into place with one of his Twist-Turn Lunges. This involved diving at the wheels at great speed, then jumping into a horizontal spin to fix the tire in place. Once that was done, Chuck added long blocks of wood to the pedals so they could control them while still being able to steer and see through the windscreen. The finishing touch was the motor, fine-tuned by Donnie.

The ninja meerkats were ready to go.

CHAPTER SIX

LIVE FROM STUDIO 66

Navigating the streets of L.A. is no easy feat, but with the help of the map on Donnie's phone, they soon found themselves outside the huge gates of the film studios. Chuck stopped the van in front of the intercom, and Jet jumped up and punched the button.

"Yes?" said a female voice.

"We're caterers," said Chuck.

"What production are you here for?" the bored-sounding woman asked.

"Evil Plots and Good Dogs," said Bruce.

"Go on in," she said. "You need
warehouse sixty-six. You can't miss it.
It has a big sixty-six on the side. If you
see sixty-five, you need to go farther. If
you see sixty-seven, you've gone too far."

The gates clicked open and Chuck drove
the van inside.

"All my favorite films were made here!
This is so exciting!" said Bruce.

"Oh yeah," said Donnie. "A load of
warehouses with numbers on them, really
exciting. Remind me to book my holiday
here next year."

Chuck parked the van alongside the
warehouse with the large 66 on the side.
The meerkats jumped out, scurried over to
the building, and peered around the corner
at the entrance. A couple of scruffily
dressed men were unpacking bits of film
equipment out of a van nearby.

"This new director seems pretty far out," said one of the men, heaving a large metal trunk out of the back of the van.

"What do you mean, dude?" said the other, giving him a hand.

"Like, just because this scene is set in a circus he's got all the crew to dress up as circus acts. Anyone who isn't dressed in circus gear isn't allowed on set while they're filming. That's pretty weird."

"Yeah, that *is* pretty weird. Hey, let's take a break. My arms are killing me." They put the trunk down.

"This is our chance," whispered Chuck.

While the men weren't looking, the meerkats dashed over to the trunk, pushed open the lid, and crammed in amongst the equipment inside.

"Come on, we'd better get moving," said the first man. "We've got to get this stuff inside and then clear the area."

"OK, OK," said the other guy.

Once the trunk had come to rest again, Bruce lifted the lid a fraction and they all peeped out.

"Wow," said Jet.

If they hadn't known otherwise, they would have been sure they were in the Ringmaster's circus tent. Everything was perfectly recreated, from the trapezes that hung from the ceiling (complete with the Von Trapeze family, who were rehearsing up above) to the sawdust on the ground. And the meerkats instantly recognized the film crew.

"The Ringmaster's got all his goons working here," said Chuck.

The clowns were present, as was Herr Flick, the knife thrower. There was also a new guy pedalling backward and forward on a unicycle, carrying a microphone on a long boom pole to keep his balance.

"Hey, there's Vin," gasped Bruce.

The actor was pacing the set, dressed as an acrobat. He was holding a script, and was practicing his lines.

"And Doris," Jet pointed out.

The dancing dog was on a director's

chair, having her fur brushed by Honor
Longlead.

"Yeah, the first scene has Vin and two
dogs in it," said Bruce, remembering what
he'd read. "I wonder where the other one is."

The Ringmaster appeared and took his
place in the center of the fake circus tent,
a sinister smile on his face.

When the lights came back on, all the security men were lying unconscious on the floor, and the president was being held by Sheffield and Grimsby, his hands tied behind his back.

"What's the meaning of this?" he demanded.

"Oh, it's quite simple," said the Ringmaster with a menacing grin. "Kidnap and ransom, Mr. President. Kidnap and ransom."

CHAPTER SEVEN

LOOK INTO MY EYES

"What do you want?" the president cried, struggling against his captors.

"Wealth, power, and control of the WORLD, of course!" the Ringmaster replied.

"Honor! Vin! Get help!" the president pleaded.

Vin merely rifled the pages of his script, looking confused, but Honor laughed.

"Help, Jim?" she replied with a smirk. "Why would I call for help when the Ringmaster has promised to pay me half the money we get for your ransom?"

The president looked defiant. "So that's it. You expect my country to pay for my life?"

"That's stage one," said the Ringmaster. "I will demand billions of dollars for your safe return and then I'll use it to run in the election to become the next President of the United States."

"Ha! Why would anyone vote for you once they find out that you kidnapped me?" scoffed the president.

The Ringmaster laughed. "Let me introduce you to my newest recruit," he said, turning to the man on the unicycle. "Hans Free—Dutch unicyclist and hypnotist extraordinaire."

"Hypnotist? You're planning on hypnotizing the whole United States? Don't make me laugh," said the president.

"If I had wanted to make you laugh, I would have introduced you to the clowns,

Mr. President," the Ringmaster replied.

"Hey, why do politicians always have such good shoes?" asked Grimsby.

"So they can *run* for election," said Sheffield.

"Quiet, you two," snapped the Ringmaster. He turned to the unicyclist. "Let's see what you can do, Hans."

"Of course," Hans replied. He pedalled over to the president, pulled a watch on a chain from his waistcoat pocket, and proceeded to swing it back and forth in front of the president's eyes.

"Your eyelids are growing heavy," Hans chanted in a soothing voice.

"What?" scoffed the president. "You
expect me to feel sleepy, then do everything
you say? This will never wo—" Suddenly, his
eyes glazed over and he fell silent.

"He's under," said Hans Free.

"Excellent. Tell him what he's going to do
after his safe return," said the Ringmaster.

"Mr. President," said Hans. "Once we
have ransomed you for billions of dollars
and you are back at the White House, you
will announce that your ordeal has made
you rethink your priorities and that you are
standing down from politics to make way
for a better man. You will tell the American
people that they should place their trust
in a new president by the name of the
Ringmaster."

"The American people should place
their trust in the Ringmaster," echoed the
president.

"The American voters will be so impressed with the way you have dealt with your kidnapping they will be ready to listen to anything you say," the Ringmaster said. "With the elections coming up, I will win by a landslide and become the most powerful man in the world."

Chip O'Lata growled angrily, but Doris leaped, snarling, into his path, keeping him at bay.

"Is this part of the film?" asked Vin Pain. "Because I can't find the page in my script."

"Oh yes, it's all part of the film, Vin," said the Ringmaster.

"Mr. Pain, it's time to throw away your script. This plot just got real," said a voice from the corner of the studio.

The Ringmaster and his cronies turned to see the four meerkats leaping out of the trunk in the corner.

"The Clan of the Scorpion! Will I never be rid of you?" snarled the Ringmaster. "Get them!"

Quick as a flash, the seven Von Trapeze children leaped into action. The older ones catapulted their younger siblings down at the meerkats from the trapezes above, then dived down themselves.

"Aren't they supposed to attack one at a time?" asked Vin, looking confused.

"This isn't a film, Vin," cried Donnie, pulling a handful of marbles from his backpack. "This is really happening. Bruce, throw me!"

Bruce ducked to avoid a kick to the head, then grabbed Donnie, spun around once, and hurled him up into the air. As he soared above their heads, Donnie threw the marbles so they scattered across the floor, tripping up three of the Von Trapezes.

The youngest boy grabbed a large roll of film and flung it at Bruce. But Bruce caught it and sent it flying toward his opponent, knocking him backward.

"That sent him *reeling*," said Jet with a smirk. He landed a roundhouse kick on

another one of the troupe. The acrobat
stumbled backward and tripped over Chip
O'Lata, who had jumped into his path.

"Good work, Chip!" Jet cheered.

The entire Von Trapeze family was now
unconscious, but Hans Free was pedalling
speedily toward the meerkats, his pocket
watch at the ready. "You are all feeling very
sleeeeepy," he said.

Chuck drew his sword. "Time to wake
up and smell the ninjas," he said, leaping
into the air and slicing clean through the
watch chain.

SLICE!

Hans grabbed a nearby boom pole with a big furry microphone on the end, and swung it at Chuck and Jet. The meerkats jumped, avoiding being knocked off their feet, then ducked to dodge it a second time.

"Talk about Ninja-boom!" said Jet.

Chuck spun around and sliced the boom pole in half, causing Hans Free to wobble precariously on his unicycle. Jet then grabbed the remaining end of the pole and swung the unicyclist around, sending him clattering into a corner.

"Now for the Ringmaster," said Chuck. "Where is he?"

"And the rest of his goons," said Donnie.

Chip O'Lata yelped and pointed at an open door on the other side of the set.

"Quick, after him!" said Chuck.

"I'm afraid I can't let you do that," said Honor, emerging from the darkness.

She put a shiny whistle to her lips and gave it a quick blow.

Suddenly, the air was filled with the sound of barking, and a pack of Dobermans raced into the room. Bud scooped Chip up in his teeth, holding the struggling sausage dog by the scruff of his neck.

The other dogs lined up around him.

"It's time for some Bruce Force," said
Bruce.

The dogs outnumbered him ten to one,
and had huge snapping jaws and powerful
legs, but they were no match for the might
of Bruce Willowhammer. As two dogs came
charging at him, he ducked and
they collided with an
almighty THUMP.
Next, Bruce
rolled into a ball
and aimed
himself at the
rest of the pack.
"Strike!" he cried, as
he knocked the dogs
over like bowling pins. He
leaped to his feet and set about kicking and
punching any that were left standing, turning
their angry barks into pathetic whimpers.

In the confusion, Donnie yanked Bud's tail. He yelped and released Chip, who ran to safety.

"Wow, I've never seen anything like that before," said Vin. "That meerkat is a *true* action hero."

Chuck smiled. "Yes. Bruce's skills in battle are quite something to behold," he agreed. Then he called, "Donnie, Bruce! Keep Chip and Vin safe. Jet and I will go after the Ringmaster."

"No problem," said Bruce, leaping onto Bud's shoulders and landing a double-fisted punch on his head, causing him to crash to the ground.

"Come, Jet," said Chuck, "it's time for a change of scene."

CHAPTER EIGHT

A CHANGE OF SCENE

Chuck and Jet hurried into the next studio and found themselves on a film set that had been made to look like a desert, with huge sand dunes and a glowing red sunset.

"It looks just like home!" Jet said.

"There they are," cried Chuck.

The Ringmaster was disappearing over a dune with Doris and Herr Flick. The two clowns were just behind them, carrying the president.

"Give it up, Ringmaster," yelled Jet. "Your plan will never work."

The Ringmaster stopped next to a large fan in front of the fake sunset and said, "Sometimes I wonder why our relationship has to be so stormy . . . *Sand*stormy, that is."

He switched the fan to maximum speed, sending huge clouds of sand at the meerkats, before disappearing through a door to the next set.

Luckily, living in the Red Desert, the meerkats had faced more than their fair share of sandstorms. Instinctively, they dived into the sand and burrowed beneath the surface, tunnelling their way across the desert until they reached the door on the other side of the studio.

The next set they stepped onto was dark and full of tiny points of light, as though they were in space. The ground was filled with craters, like the surface of the moon, and large planets were hanging from the ceiling.

"Hey uh, Grimsby, this set is *out of this world*," said Sheffield.

Grimsby slid his feet backward along the ground. "Yeah, look at me. I'm *moonwalking*."

"Stop messing around," said the Ringmaster. "Herr Flick—time to put an end to our unwelcome globe-trotters."

"Now, *das meerkätzchen* will be flattened!" said Herr Flick.

He pulled a knife from his belt and lobbed it at a rope that was suspending a huge red planet from the ceiling. The massive sphere crashed to the ground and thundered toward the meerkats.

"You're in a *world* of trouble now," cackled Grimsby.

"The Way of the Scorpion teaches us that even the smallest creature can move a planet so long as he has a place to stand," replied Chuck.

He rammed his sword into the ground and bowed down. Jet ducked too, just in time; the planet hit the sword and shot up over them.

Chuck stood up to see that, once again, the Ringmaster had fled through an exit. But this one led outside, where a helicopter was starting up, its propellers gathering speed. The Ringmaster and Doris were already on board, and Herr Flick was in the pilot's seat. The clowns bundled the president inside and climbed in just before the helicopter took off.

"We are too late!" said Chuck.

"We could always hitch a ride," said a voice behind them.

Donnie, Bruce, Chip O'Lata, and Vin Pain appeared around the corner of the building. Donnie was holding a harpoon, which he threw at the helicopter, looping the grappling hook onto one of its landing skids.

"The security guys woke up just after we got the dogs under control," Donnie explained. "So we thought we'd catch up with you. The security team were planning to contact the U.S. Army, but we're going to need to slow the Ringmaster down to buy them some time."

The meerkats grabbed hold of the end of the rope, and waited to be lifted into the air.

Chip O'Lata joined them, biting down on the rope and looking determined.

"I'm coming too. I'm fed up of just acting like a hero. I want to be one—like you guys," said Vin Pain, grabbing hold of the rope just in time for the helicopter to whisk them all off the ground.

CHAPTER NINE

A SIGN OF THE TIMES

The helicopter flew over L.A., trailing a rope that carried a well-known action star, the president's sausage dog, and four meerkats.

"I can't believe I'm doing this," Vin Pain bellowed, his eyes shut tight.

"But you do all your own stunts," Bruce shouted up. "What about that time you held onto a helicopter in *Big Guns and Loud Bangs 3*?"

"I was two feet off the ground when we filmed that!" he replied.

The side door of the helicopter opened

and Sheffield leaned out. "Hey! It's time for all of you to *sign off*!" he shouted.

They looked ahead and saw that the helicopter was flying low over the hills . . . sending them speeding toward the enormous Hollywood sign.

Vin opened his eyes. "Look out!" he cried.

"Swing the rope!" Chuck ordered. "Left first!"

Everyone leaned to the left.

"Now to the right!" yelled Chuck.

The rope swung like a pendulum, getting higher and higher with each push. Just in the nick of time, they built up enough momentum to swing the rope wide of the sign. They whizzed past the letter "Y", mere millimeters from their doom.

Then the helicopter turned around and headed back toward the sign.

"Jet, this is a perfect opportunity to use

the Super Looping Somersault Leap," said Chuck. "Everyone else, we're close enough to the ground now to jump safely. Let go of the rope when I count to three. One, two, three!"

What came next happened so fast, it was little more than a blur. While Jet hung onto the rope, the others dropped to the ground. As the helicopter approached one of the "O"s, Jet swung straight through the center of it, then up and over the top of the letter, and back through the hole, again and again, until the rope was tightly secured. Jet then leaped safely to the ground.

"Now that's what I call a Super Looping Somersault Leap!" he cheered.

The helicopter tried to pull away, but it was well and truly stuck. Moments later, it began to lose control.

"Abandon helicopter!" cried the Ringmaster. He, Doris, Herr Flick, and the clowns, carrying the president, jumped to safety just before the abandoned helicopter crashed to the ground and exploded.

"Everything *always* explodes in Hollywood," Donnie sighed, shaking his head.

"Get them, you fools!" cried the Ringmaster.

Vin raised his fists. "Things are getting rough around here . . . so I'm about to get tough!"

Herr Flick drew a knife and took aim. "As they say in the movies, cut!" he said, lobbing the knife at the actor.

But Bruce leaped at Vin, pushing him out of harm's way.

"Thanks," said Vin, looking shaken.

Meanwhile, the clowns both pulled out guns with enormous barrels.

Chuck drew his sword. "How about you pick on someone who *isn't* your own size," he said. "Before the Clan, each enemy cowers, for now we fight till victory is ours."

"Hey, Sheffield," said Grimsby. "If only

my mother could see me now, in Hollywood
on a *shoot*... She'd be so proud."

The clowns pulled the triggers, and
creamy white disk-shaped missiles shot at
the meerkats.

"Exploding cream pies!" exclaimed
Donnie, diving out of the way.

"Ninja-boom!"
yelled Jet, dodging
the cream pie. He
sprang back up and
kicked Sheffield in
the stomach, sending
him staggering
backward.

"That's a waste of good food," said
Bruce. He kicked at Grimsby's legs so that
he crumpled to the ground, then reached
out and grabbed a handful of cream pie
that had landed nearby.

Meanwhile, Chuck made short work of Herr Flick, knocking him down and using his own knives to pin him to the ground.

Donnie charged at Doris. She jumped up, spun around, and snapped at him, but he dodged her jaws and executed a high kick that sent her flying.

"You should've stuck to acting," he said.

Farther up the hill, the Ringmaster was trying to make his getaway, the hypnotized president in tow, when a snarling Chip O'Lata appeared in front of him.

"Out of my way," sneered the Ringmaster. "You think I'm scared of a dog named after a party snack?"

Chip growled angrily and lunged at the Ringmaster, but he kicked him away, sending the dog tumbling down the hill.

"Hey, it's a *sausage roll*," sniggered Grimsby, freeing Herr Flick.

"Yep, the *chips* are definitely down now," said Sheffield.

As Vin leaped to Chip's aid, catching the dizzy dog in his arms, a strange juddering sound filled the air.

Chuck looked up, and smiled at the sight of the approaching twin-propeller helicopters. "Look, Ringmaster!" yelled Chuck. "The U.S. Army is coming. Your evil plot will never succeed. Release the president!"

"You wretched meerkats!" the Ringmaster cried. "One day I will defeat you and the world will be mine. Sheffield, Grimsby, Doris, Herr Flick—it's time we left. I think this president's career is about to go downhill." And with that, he pushed the president away, sending him tumbling down the slope after his dog.

Vin got himself into position again and caught the president, who looked dazed and confused. The tumble down the hill seemed to have broken him out of his hypnotized state.

"We can't let the Ringmaster get away!" cried Jet, as the two clowns sent a shower of exploding cream pies into the air to cover their escape. But his voice could barely be heard above the sound of the helicopters.

"Nobody move," said a voice from above. "This is the United States Military."

"We must go too," said Chuck. "We can only hope the military is quick enough to capture the Ringmaster."

"What!" Jet wailed. "Surely, we can take the credit for this one."

"It is not our way," said Chuck. He looked at the president, who was patting his beloved dog. "Chip has his master back, the Ringmaster has been defeated, and the president is safe. The Clan of the Scorpion's work is done."

Vin ran over and joined them. "You guys aren't leaving, are you?" he panted.

"I'm afraid so, Mr. Pain," said Chuck. "And we would appreciate it if you didn't mention us in the recounting of this adventure."

"What should I say?" asked Vin.

"That is entirely up to you."

"Meeting you was one of the most exciting things that has ever happened to me," said Bruce.

"The pleasure was all mine," Vin replied.

With a simple bow, the ninja meerkats disappeared into the undergrowth, unseen by the circling helicopters.

CHAPTER TEN

WORKING TITLES

After leaving Vin, Chip, and the president, the meerkats made their way back to the studio and retrieved the hot-dog van. They drove to a nearby suburb and parked it on a residential street for the night.

"We should stay in town for a little while longer," said Chuck. "See if we can pick up any more news of the Ringmaster."

"And maybe squeeze in a little sightseeing too," said Bruce hopefully.

After an uncomfortable night's sleep in the back of the van, Chuck, Jet, and Bruce were woken by Donnie, who was watching a news report on his mobile phone.

"Check this out," said Donnie, turning up the volume.

"In a story straight from a film plot, there was a bold attempt to kidnap the president yesterday, which was thwarted by none other than action star Vin Pain and the president's own dog, Chip O'Lata."

"I can't believe they took all the credit," moaned Jet.

"The man behind the plot was the director and producer of Vin Pain's latest film, *Evil Plots and Good Dogs*. Very little is known about him except that he goes by the name of 'the Ringmaster.' Authorities say he is still at large. Celebrity dog trainer Honor Longlead has also been arrested in connection with the plot."

The phone's screen showed Honor being

led away by the police, as hordes of flashing cameras took her picture, then the report moved on to another news story.

"Can we go sightseeing now?" asked Bruce.

"On one condition: You act as our tour guide," said Chuck. "After all, on this mission it was you who proved to be the expert."

"Excellent!" Bruce exclaimed with a grin.

"Hey, do you think they'll make a film about us one day?" asked Donnie.

"Yeah, called something like *Jet Flashfeet: Ninja-boom!*" suggested Jet.

"No way," argued Bruce. "It'd be called *Bruce Willowhammer: Force of Nature.*"

"I think *Enter the Dragonjab* is a pretty good title," said Donnie.

"Yeah, right," Jet and Bruce chorused.

"There could never be a film of our exploits," said Chuck. "Secrecy, discretion, and humility are key to our success."

The others groaned.

"But if there was a film," he added with a smile, "it would probably be called *Chuck Cobracrusher: King of Ninjas.*"

"Of course!" Donnie replied, as Jet and Bruce laughed. "Come on—we've got sights to see."

"And snacks to sample," added Bruce. "Let's go!"

This time, the meerkats must race to a burial chamber deep within an Egyptian pyramid in order to protect a legendary golden mask from the clutches of the evil Ringmaster!

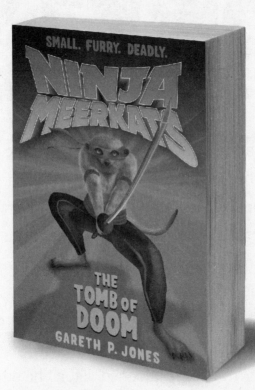

Find out if they succeed in

Ninja Meerkats:
The Tomb of Doom

CHAPTER ONE

A LOB DISTANCE CALL

It had been almost a month since the Clan of the Scorpion last encountered their deadly enemy the Ringmaster and his circus goons. They were enjoying a welcome break from saving the world back at their secret underground base in the Red Desert.

Or, at least, three of them were enjoying the break.

"I'm bored," moaned Jet, as he entered the main chamber of their burrow, trailing his nunchucks behind him.

"You could give me a hand with this,"

said Donnie, who was struggling with
something flat, rectangular, and twice
his size.

Bruce looked up from his bag of dry-
roasted crickets. "What is that?" he asked.

"It's our new TV," said Donnie proudly,
placing it on a table by the wall. "It's got a
high-definition plasma screen and surround-
sound speakers. Welcome to the future, my
friends."

Chuck, who had been meditating silently
in the corner, opened one eye. "Why do we
need such a thing?" he asked. "We would
only use it for keeping up with what is
happening in the outside world, and we
can already do that through the Internet."

"Ah, but it also has a Web cam," said
Donnie. "That means that once I've hooked it
up, we'll be able to receive video calls on the
big screen instead of on my smartphone!"

He pulled a remote control and some cables
from his pocket, and connected the TV to
the power and the router.

"Hey, we could watch action films on it
too!" Bruce pointed out. "Vin Pain has got
a new movie out—it's called *Lethal Biscuit
Two: Redunked*."

"Films are no substitute for the real
thing," said Jet, spinning around and
whacking a punching bag. "I'm *so bored*."

"You should be using this time for quiet
meditation and practicing the art of kung
fu, Jet," said Chuck. "Haven't you a new
technique to work on?"

"Well, I *was* trying to learn one called
the Squeeze of Rigidity," said Jet.

"That sounds cool," said Bruce. "What
is it?"

"It's a move that causes your opponent's
muscles to freeze, putting them out of

action temporarily," Jet replied. "But my kung-fu manual went missing."

"You can borrow this one," said an elderly voice. "It is most entertaining."

Grandmaster One-Eye entered the chamber, clutching a book.

"Hey," exclaimed Jet. "That *is* my book!"

"Oh, is it?" asked the ancient meerkat. "Well, it's reminded me about some of the moves I used to do. When you get to my age, the jogging of one's memory is just about the only kind of jogging you can manage." He smiled and handed it to Jet.

"Did you ever perform the Squeeze of Rigidity, Grandmaster?" Jet asked.

"Oh yes, I was something of an expert at that one in my day."

"Would you demonstrate it for me?" asked Jet excitedly. "I've been practicing, but I can't work out how hard you need to—"

Grandmaster One-Eye reached out his paw and gently squeezed Jet's arm, cutting him short. Jet fell backward, his body completely rigid. Bruce jumped up and caught him just before he crashed to the floor.

"'ot 'id you 'o 'hat 'or?" mumbled Jet.

"Well, you did ask him to demonstrate the move," said Chuck with a wry smile. "And at least you're not bored anymore."

"No," Donnie laughed. "Now he's as *stiff* as a board."

Jet groaned.

"How long will he be like this for?" asked Bruce, laying him gently on the ground.

"Feeling will return to his body gradually over the next few hours," said One-Eye, looking quite pleased with himself.

"A 'ew 'ours?" Jet exclaimed.

"I believe the toes regain feeling first. He'll be as right as rain soon enough," the Grandmaster assured them. "The Squeeze of Rigidity, eh? Who would have thought I still had the knack!"

A ringing sound suddenly echoed around the burrow.

"What's that?" asked Bruce.

"An incoming call," said Donnie. "We can try out the new Web cam!"

Donnie clicked the remote control and a single eye appeared on the enormous TV. The owner of the eye moved back to reveal a meerkat bearing a striking resemblance to Chuck, standing in a tunnel and wearing a sand-colored robe.

"It's my brother, Lob," said Chuck. "Lob, it has been too long! How is Cairo?"

"Greetings to you, Chuck," said Lob hurriedly. "I am afraid this is not a social call. I need your help."

"Grillian'!" said Jet.

"What did he say?" asked Lob.

"Don't ask," said Chuck. "What do you need help with?"

Lob checked over his shoulder, then whispered, "It is not safe for me to explain over a video call. Please come to Cairo and I will tell you everything."

"We will catch the next flight out," promised Chuck. "How will we find you when we get there?"

"Just tell me when you are due to arrive and I'll find you," said Lob. "Please hurry."

The screen went blank and Chuck turned to the others. "We have a mission."

"So, you're off to Egypt, eh? I once fought the Crazy Camels of Cairo there," said Grandmaster One-Eye with a wistful smile.

"Really? How did you defeat them?" asked Chuck.

"Oh, they were no match for my moves." One-Eye demonstrated with a karate chop that accidentally knocked over a row of fighting staffs. "Eventually they got the hump and ran off."

Donnie sniggered, but Chuck bowed respectfully. "You are indeed a worthy adversary, Grandmaster. But if you will excuse us, we must be on our way. Bruce, bring Jet. To the Meer-kart!"

GO**FISH**

Gareth P. Jones

What did you want to be when you grew up?
At various points, a writer, a musician, an intergalactic bounty hunter and, for a limited period, a graphic designer. (I didn't know what that meant, but I liked the way it sounded.)

When did you realize you wanted to be a writer?
I don't remember realizing it. I have always loved stories. From a very young age, I enjoyed making them up. As I'm not very good at making things up on the spot, this invariably involved having to write them down.

What's your most embarrassing childhood memory?
Seriously? There are too many. I have spent my entire life saying and doing embarrassing things. Just thinking about some of them is making me cringe. Luckily, I have a terrible memory, so I can't remember them all, but no, I'm not going to write any down for you. If I did that, I'd never be able to forget them.

What's your favorite childhood memory?
To be honest with you, I don't remember my childhood very well at all (I told you I had a bad memory), but I do recall how my dad used to tell me stories. He would make them up as he went along, most likely borrowing all sorts of elements from the books he was reading without me knowing.

As a young person, who did you look up to most?
My mom and dad, Prince, Michael Jackson, all of Monty Python, and Stephen Fry.

What was your favorite thing about school?
Laughing with my friends.

What was your least favorite thing about school?
I had a bit of a hard time when I moved from the Midlands to London at the age of twelve because I had a funny accent. But don't worry, it was all right in the end.

What were your hobbies as a kid? What are your hobbies now?
I love listening to and making music. My hobbies haven't really changed over the years, except that there's a longer list of instruments now. When I get a chance, I like idling away the day playing trumpet, guitar, banjo, ukulele, mandolin (and piano if there's one in the vicinity). I also like playing out with my friends.

What was your first job, and what was your "worst" job?

My first job was working as a waiter. That's probably my worst job, too. As my dad says, I was a remarkably grumpy waiter. I'm not big on all that serving-people malarkey.

What book is on your nightstand now?

I have a pile of books from my new publisher. I'm trying to get through them before I meet the authors. I'm half-way through *Maggot Moon* by Sally Gardner, which is written in the amazing voice of a dyslexic boy.

How did you celebrate publishing your first book?

The first time I saw one of my books in a shop, I was so excited that I caused something of a commotion. I managed to persuade an unsuspecting customer to buy it so I could sign it for her son.

Where do you write your books?

Anywhere and everywhere. Here are some of the locations I have written the Ninja Meerkats series: On the 185 and the 176 buses in London, various airplanes, Hong Kong, Melbourne, all over New Zealand, a number of cafes and bars between San Diego and San Francisco, New Quay in South Wales, and my kitchen.

What sparked your imagination for the Ninja Meerkats?

The idea came from the publishing house, but from the moment I heard it, I really wanted to write it. It reminded me of lots of action-packed cartoons I used to watch when I was young. I love the fact that I get to cram in lots of jokes and puns, fast action, and crazy outlandish plots.

The Ninja Meerkats are awesome fighters; have you ever studied martial arts? If so, what types?
Ha, no. If I was to get into a fight, my tactic would be to fall over and hope that whoever was attacking me lost interest.

If you were a Ninja Meerkat, what would your name be?
Hmm, how about Gareth *POW!* Jones?

What's your favorite exhibit or animal at the zoo?
Funnily enough, I like the meerkats. I was at a zoo watching them the other day when it started to rain. They suddenly ran for cover, looking exactly like their human visitors.

What's Bruce's favorite food?
Anything with the words ALL YOU CAN EAT written above it.

If you had a catchphrase like Bruce Force! or Ninja-Boom! what would it be?
That's a tricky one. How about PEN POWER!

If you were a Ninja Meerkat, what would your special ninja skill be?
I like to think I'd be like Jet, and always working on a new one. When I got into school, I took the Random Move

Generator! We used it to come up with new moves, like the Floating Butterfly Punch and the Ultimate Lemon Punch.

What is your favorite thing about real-life meerkats? Have you ever met a meerkat?
I was lucky enough to go into a meerkat enclosure recently. They were crawling all over me, trying to get a good view. It was brilliant.

What challenges do you face in the writing process, and how do you overcome them?
The challenge with writing the Ninja Meerkats books is mostly about the plotting. It's trying to get all the twists and turns to work, and to avoid them feeling predictable. When I hit problems, I write down as many options as I can think of from the completely ordinary to utterly ridiculous. Once they're all down on paper, the right answer normally jumps out at you.

Which of your characters is most like you?
I'd like to say that I'm wise and noble like Chuck, but I'm probably more like the Ringmaster as we're both always coming up with new ways to take over the world.

What makes you laugh out loud?
My friends.

What do you do on a rainy day?
Play guitar, write, watch TV, or go out with my sword-handled umbrella.

What's your idea of fun?
Answering questionnaires about myself. Actually, tomorrow, I'm going to a music festival with my wife where we will dance and cavort. That should be fun.

What's your favorite song?
There are far too many to mention, but today I think I'll go for "Feel Good Inc." by Gorillaz.

Who is your favorite fictional character?
Another tricky one, but today I'll say Ged from the Earthsea Trilogy by Ursula K. Le Guin.

What was your favorite book when you were a kid? Do you have a favorite book now?
As a child, I especially loved *The Phantom Tollbooth* by Norton Juster.

What's your favorite TV show or movie?
Raiders of the Lost Ark.

If you were stranded on a desert island, who would you want for company?
My wife and son, then probably my friend Pete, as he's really handy and would be able to make and build things.

If you could travel anywhere in the world, where would you go and what would you do?
I'd like to go to Canada next. Ideally, I'd like to go and live there for a bit. I've never been to South America. There are also lots of parts of America I haven't visited yet.

SQUARE FISH

If you could travel in time, where would you go and what would you do?
I think I'd travel to the future and see what's changed and whether anyone's invented a new kind of umbrella.

What's the best advice you have ever received about writing?
Don't tell the story, show the story.

What advice do you wish someone had given you when you were younger?
Everything's probably going to be fine, so it's best to enjoy yourself.

Do you ever get writer's block? What do you do to get back on track?
It feels like tempting fate, but I don't really believe in writer's block. I think if you can't write, you're doing the wrong thing. You may need to plan or jot down options or go for a walk.

What do you want readers to remember about your books?
I'd settle for a general feeling of having enjoyed them.

What would you do if you ever stopped writing?
I'd do a full stop. If this is for an American audience, I guess that would be a period.

What should people know about you?
I'm a very silly man.

SQUARE FISH

What do you like best about yourself?
I'm a very silly man.

Do you have any strange or funny habits? Did you when you were a kid?
I talk to myself a lot, which is probably pretty common, but the difference is that I don't listen to what I'm saying.